McGill University

McGill University: annual graduates' dinner

McGill University

McGill University: annual graduates' dinner

Reprint of the original, first published in 1879.

1st Edition 2024 | ISBN: 978-3-38800-252-1

Antigonos Verlag is an imprint of Outlook Verlagsgesellschaft mbH.

Verlag (Publisher): Outlook Verlag GmbH, Zeilweg 44, 60439 Frankfurt, Deutschland, info@outlook-verlag.de
Vertretungsberechtigt (Authorized to represent): E. Roepke, Zeilweg 44, 60439 Frankfurt, Deutschland
Druck (Print): Libri Plureos GmbH, Friedensallee 273, 22763 Hamburg, Deutschland

McGILL UNIVERSITY

ANNUAL GRADUATES' DINNER

1879

McGILL UNIVERSITY.

ANNUAL GRADUATES' DINNER.

The Annual University Dinner under the auspices of the McGill College Graduates, which came off in the Ladies' Ordinary, at the Windsor Hotel, last evening, was attended with much *éclat*. Nearly two hundred persons sat down to the well-laid tables, shortly after 8 o'clock, and partook of a repast furnished in the Windsor's best style. Mr. J. S. Hall, Jr., in the absence of Mr. J. S. McLennan, President of the Graduates' Society, occupied the Chair, and was supported on his right by Principal Dawson, C.M.G., Dr. R. P. Howard, Dean of the Faculty of Medicine, Mr. John Molson, Dr. H. A. Howe, Mr. R. A. Ramsay, Hon. L. R. Church, and on his left by Hon. Chancellor Heneker, of Bishop's College, Hon. Justice Johnson, Hon. R. Stearns, U. S. Consul-General, and Rev. Dr. Stevenson. The vice chairs were occupied by Dr. W. A. Molson, and Prof. McLeod, and among the large number present were noticed Dr. Alex. Johnson, Rev. Dr. Murray, Rev. Prof. Cornoirat, Dr. Ross. Dr. Gardner, Dr. Girdwood, Dr. Rodger, Dr. Bell, Dr. Osler and Dr. Wilkins, Mr. Kennedy, Harbor Engineer, Dr. F. W. Kelly, Prof. Moyse, Hugh Graham, J. N. Greenshields, C. J. Fleet, John McLean, Rev. T. Lafleur, Joseph Rielle, S. Sheldon Stephens, Moses Davis, W. McLennan, Francis McLennan, Dr. R. Macdonnell, L. N. Benjamin, R. D. McGibbon, P. A. Peterson, J. E. Robidoux, N. W. Trenholme, C. A. Geoffrion, Louis Frechette, John J. MacLaren, H. J. Kavanagh, C. Beausoleil, — Bisaillon, H. Beaugrand, O. H. Stephens, J. S. Archibald, M. Hutchinson, Alex. Weir, A. W. Smith, K. Macpherson, N. T. Rielle, G. H. Chandler, O. Cushing, R. Stirling, Frederick Hague, Harry Hague, C. Duclos, Rev. Mr. Newnham, Eugene Lafleur, W. F. Ritchie, M. S. Loosenan, J. L. Morin, H. M. Aime, Jeffrey H. Burland, W. McLea Walbank, W. M. Taylor, Roswell Fisher, H. H. Lyman,

A. C. Lyman, G. Couture, — Racine, — Greenshields, Reg. Kennedy, Dr. Shepherd, and many others.

After the excellent *menu* had been partaken of to the satisfaction of all, the bugle was sounded, and the President arose and proposed the first toast of the evening, "The Queen," which was most loyally and enthusiastically honoured, all present joining in singing the National Anthem.

The toast of "The Governor-General" was also enthusiastically honoured amid cheers

Mr. K. Macpherson then gave a song in an excellent manner which was loudly *encored.*

"OUR UNIVERSITY."

The Chairman, Mr. J. S. Hall, in proposing the toast of the evening, "Our University," said:—"I regret, gentleman, on this occasion the absence of our President, who should have proposed the next toast. As one of the next in office the lot has fallen upon me, and I can assure you it is an honour of which I am proud, though I feel little able to do justice to the toast. Coming from a body of graduates there seems to be no more fitting toast than that of their University, yet at the same time it requires but little introduction. (Applause.) In looking at our programme and seeing the name of our Principal, who is to respond, I feel my weakness. The able University lecture, recently delivered by him, gives such a full account of the University, its history with the trials and struggles, and the results that have been obtained, that little more can be said. We can, however, as graduates look back and be proud of our Alma Mater. (Applause.) When we consider the small nucleus she sprang from, surrounded with a litigation that threatened her existence and yet see her emerge and grow, nurtured by friends of which she can be proud, and with resolute men at the helm, we may well have a feeling ot satisfaction. (Applause.) During all this period, situated in this city, though the commercial metropolis, her aims and teachings were all broad, and have never been local. As a result to-day she stands not with a local character, not with a sectarian name, but with a broad national fame and reputation. (Applause.) Go where one will, her reputation is known, her solid educational basis admitted, and in comparison with any of the Universities on this continent, or even on the other, few will stand a better criticism than McGill of Canada. (Continued applause.) Well, gentlemen. we must maintain this reputation, and use our best energies and exertions to always preserve it. I am not going to do any begging or anything that might seem like begging. The University has many friends, and in looking at our list of benefactors, we can boast of many tried and valued supporters. I question, too, if we consider the age of our Alma Mater and the individual wealth of our community that either of the two great American Universities of Harvard and Yale, could show better educational record. (Applause.) Yet, while we are congratulating ourselves, we must not forget the advancing requirements of any system of education, and the means necessary to carry them on. Within a comparatively few years we can observe in our University the addition of a Faculty of Applied Science, the increase in the Faculty of Medicine, the extensions in the various musuems and laboratories, in the observatory, and also the change in the curriculum of the Faculty of Arts, by which greater specialties may be obtained. I must not forget to mention the question of the higher education of women, now before the Corporation, and the advisability of their admission to the educational advantages of the Faculty of Arts. (Applause.) All these matters have forced themselves on the University, not particularly on this University, but upon every educational Institution, if it means to maintain its efficiency. They are all important, and require serious consideration. Education is continually advancing in our state of society, and requires greater means and support. It is not the interest of any one in particular, but the interest of all, that this must be given. Well, gentlemen, about this main support we can rely in the future on the generous friends of the Universities. (Applause.) The same spirit still exists in this city, and our friends will always see that the fair name of McGill will never be impaired for want of their support. (Continued applause.) In referring to ourselves as graduates, we mu t not forget what we can do. I recollect a few years ago when several graduates met together to consider the advisability of forming this society. The objects by some were misunderstood, and it was thought a body was being formed of a radical order, and perhaps to work antagonistic to the interests of the University, but I am happy to say that they were mistaken. There was and had been a feeling for a long time among the graduates, that year after year numbers of them went forth from the University, and little if any means existed of keeping them together, and securing their interest in the University. And thus in their leaving a great support was lost. The formation of the society was agreed upon, and so far the results have been satisfactory. (Applause.) The society has been regularly maintained, and though young we have contributed our mite to the various libraries. We have also discussed subjects before the Corporation, and the changes that might be made. This has been done in a proper spirit and with a feeling that if any discussion arose it was far better to discuss it in a constituted body. No institution can stand without some discussion, without some changes, and it is more healthy to have this come from within the institution than from without, and by the graduates, who have, perhaps, greater interest at heart in the University than any others. We have also started a fund for a donation of some kind to the University. To those who have passed through any of the Faculties, and especially those students who came from the country, there is no greater want felt than that of a lodging or dining hall adjacent to the lecture rooms. (Applause). The loss of time, the inconvenience, and I must add, the discomforts that have been borne, if capable of capitalizing in money, would, long ago, have erected this building, and, if we can only succeed now in realizing the object, these wasted energies in the future could be devoted to better purposes. I wish earnestly to appeal to the graduates to assist in this. It means but a little for all, but that all should join. If we can't succeed as far as this, the fund will be devoted to some building. In searching for a name it was decided, when finished, to call it the Dawson Hall. (Loud applause). As a body of graduates it was recognized that in the Principal there was one who had done yeoman's service for the University, and it was the least tribute and mark of gratitude we could offer him in asking that it should bear I is name. Gentlemen, before I sit down I wish you all to join me in offering to that gentlemen our best wishes during his leave of absence. After a service of more than a quarter of a century in the interests of the University, in the interests of the community at a continual self-sacrifice, a year's leave of absence is a well earned rest, in which the least we can do is to offer him every happiness, every joy and a safe return. [Loud and continued applause].

The toast was honoured in a most enthusiastic manner, those present singing "For He's a Jolly Good Fellow."

Dr. Frechette, the Poet Laureate, was then called upon and recited, in a most eloquent manner, one of his poems.

<h3>DR. DAWSON'S REPLY.</h3>

Principal Dawson, on rising to respond to the toast, was greeted with loud and long continued applause, which lasted for some minutes. When the enthusiasm occasioned by his appearance had subsided, Principal Dawson returned thanks to those present for their kindness, and paid a high compliment to the poet laureate, Dr. Frechette. He referred in humourous terms to the fact that he had always been called upon to respond to this toast, and expressed the hope from what had been said that on his return next year he might respond to the toast of " The Lady Graduates." (Laughter and applause.) During the evening he said a gentleman had propounded to him the question whether it was the hotels or the university that had made the greatest progress during the last twenty-five years. (Laughter and applause.) He thought that they might say at any rate that the University movement had made just as great progress as the hotel movement which culminated in the Windsor. [Applause.] But there was a difference, he would like them to remember, between the two institutions,—the one was for the generation in which it existed, but the University had to keep pace with the present, and point forward to something nobler and greater. [Loud applause.] The University should be the vanguard of advancement and ever look forward to the future. [Applause.] He next referred in happy terms to the medals which had been presented by Dr. Wickstead, of Ottawa, for physical training. [Applause.] He believed that these medals were indicative of one great principle in their University work—that was that it had always been their aim to give a general and comprehensive culture and not seek to make the pupils either doctors, lawyers or ministers alone. (Applause.) He believe this was the true function of the University. He referred to the great importance of physical training. The University, he said, was not for the purpose of cramming men and filling their heads with a mass of facts, but their aim had been to give that broad liberal culture which would make the students mental facilities as supple and active as the trained athelete's muscles. The aim of the University had been to train to the fullest extent the mental facilities of the students. That which they might term the scientific training of the mind, was now receiving greater attention, and he believed that the true aim of the University should be to develop the power of mind that is in the student, and, therefore, enable him to be the more powerful, influential and useful member of society. He did not speak of their moral education, but in his opinion it was impossible to give a sound scientific culture to men without giving them a bias towards that which is good and true. [Applause.] The work of the University was a practical one and was becoming more and more practical as time went on and the country progressed. The workmanship of the University was to be seen in its graduates. [Applause.] The work was a more difficult one than might at first be imagined. He hoped that the graduates would do all in their power to advance the interests of McGill. (Applause.) As their graduates became older, and more influential men, the University would look to them to do for her what other men, many of whom have not received a University education, had done for her in the past. (Loud Applause.) The time would come when these men would pass away, and the positions of trust and honour in the community would be accepted by the graduates of McGill, who would then have to support their Alma Mater. He hoped that the day was not far distant when they would see even grander and better things, and when it could be said that thanks to those who have received a higher education in the University there would be very few illiterate people in the Dominion.

Principal Dawson resumed his seat amid loud and enthusiastic applause.

OTTAWA'S GREETING.

The Chairman then read the following telegram which he had just received from Ottawa:—

Chairman University Dinner, Montreal:

The Graduates in Ottawa to their brethren in Montreal send greeting.

R. J. WICKSTEAD.

OUR SISTER UNIVERSITIES.

Mr. J. J. McLaren, Q.C., in proposing the toast of "The Sister Universities," referred to the numerous bequests, amounting in all to about one-third of a million of dollars, that the University had received of late years. [Applause.] They could also rejoice for the prosperity that had been attending all the universities of this Province and of the Dominion, Laval, Bishops' College, Queens and Victoria College. [Applause.] They had also with them a distinguished graduate of one of the most distinguished American Colleges, that of Princeton. [Applause.] A college that during the presidency of Principal McCosh had received benefactions to the amount of over two and a half million of dollars. [Applause.]

The toast was enthusiastically honoured, after which Mr. N. T. Rielle gave a song in excellent manner.

CHANCELLOR HENNEKER'S ADDRESS.

Hon. Chancellor Henneker, in responding to the toast, expressed the great pleasure he always took in meeting the graduates of McGill. Though not one of the graduates, he was heart and soul with them in their work. (Loud applause.) That work was the great work of education. [Applause.] The University over which he was Chancellor was a very small one, but though it was small, he believed that it would not be gainsaid that the work they did was done thoroughly (Loud applause). He next referred to the fact that the degree of colleges was not a sufficient guarantee for the admission of candidates to the study of the professions in this Province. He said, as a member of the Council of Public Instruction that they had a superhuman work to do with very little means (Applause). This task was to raise the whole tone of the public school system (Applause). They found themselves at present with a system of high school education which was very efficient in the city, but very deficient in the rural districts, and hence it became their duty to raise the tone of the schools in these districts (Applause). They were met in their endeavours by the narrow prejudices of the profes-

sional men of this Province. He asked them if it was not time for them to join with the Council of Public Instruction in providing the desired improvements. (Applause.) These prejudices arose from the fact that they were incorporated bodies and desired to shut themselves off. The plan of the Council was to have an examining board, whose duty it would be to see if those who wished to enter for the study were qualified to do so, and they would never raise the standard of their country schools until they had such an examining board. The university degree, even which should stamp a man as one of culture and refinement, was not taken as a guarantee, and these men even for professional certificates in this Province were obliged to undergo examination He believed that this was a disgrace and should be fought until it no longer existed. (Applause) He did not see, if this continued, that there was any use of having a Faculty of Arts at all in this country. He wished them therefore all to join in having this obnoxious system repealed at the next session of the Quebec Legislature, and the degree to serve as a sufficient guarantee for the entrance to the study of the professions, without further examination. (Loud Applause)

United States Consul-General Stearns, in responding to the toast expressed his pleasure, as a graduate of Princeton, in being called upon to speak to this toast. He referred to the foundation of the colleges in the neighbouring republic. Within twenty years after the landing of the Pilgrim Fathers at Plymouth, Harvard University was established and then followed the foundation of Yale, Princeton and other colleges, and during the war of independence these colleges had taken a leading part. Among those who signed the declaration of independence was a graduate of his own college, James Madison, afterwards President of the United States. [Applause.] From these colleges the United States had received its greatest strength and owed to them much of its development, [Applause]. He felt that the strength and future progress of their great republic depended, to a great extent, upon the men that went out from these institutions. (Loud applause.) On behalf of these colleges of his native land, their professors and alumni, he offered them his most hearty congratulations. He concluded his eloquent remarks by referring in high terms to Principal Dawson and the valuable work he had rendered to his country and the world, in the science of geology, which was the sister science of religion. (Loud applause).

OUR OLDEST FACULTY.

Hon. L. R. Church next proposed the toast of "Our Oldest Faculty," and, in doing so, referred to the early history of the Medical Faculty and the services rendered by such men as Robertson, Holmes, and others — (applause,] and later on by the late lamented Dr. Campbell. In those early days the foundation of a medical school was no trifling matter when all the difficulties were considered. Passing on to later days, when such men as Macdonell, Hall, and others, were connected with the University, they came to modern days, the days of men now, living the days of such men as the Howards and Scotts. [Applause.] Still further changes were now about to be made, and he was assured that those who would come after would do honour to the University. [Applause.] Besides these they had the great body of graduates, who were all working for the advancement of their common profession, and who occupied positions of honour and trust in the community. [Applause.] There was one thing, however, that had so far been denied them, and that was a Governorship of the University, and he hoped that the time was not far distant when one of their profession would be made one of the Governors of the University. [Loud applause.]

Dr. R. P. Howard, Dean of the Faculty of Medicine, in responding referred to the position that the Faculty of Medicine had attained in the past. During the 30 years in which he had been connected with the University, fourteen members of the Faculty of Medicine had ceased their connection with the University, while the Faculty of Arts only lost two. The great characteristic of the Faculty in the past had been earnestness, faithfulness and regularity in the discharge of its duty. (Applause.) As their present professors had, with few exceptions, been trained in this school, he was confident that their work in the future would be marked by the same characteristics. (Applause.) For the future they had reason for hope. (Applause.) They desired to get the best and most earnest men. The Medical Faculty had been alive to the improvements that had been made in the teaching of medicine, and had acted accordingly. (Applause.) In 1870 the first great advance was made, when the student was obliged to undergo a practical examination at the bedside, and in 1876 another step forward was made when the summer session was established. (Applause.) In 1878 and '79 the Demonstrator of Anatomy was made an Examiner, and that subject was made a subject of examination, while about the same time a laboratory of physiology was established and a demonstrator appointed. These were proofs of the great advancement that this Faculty was making (applause). And now another great step was being taken in the establishment of the Campbell Endowment Fund, with a view to enlarging their sphere of usefulness and also the establishment of a new chair (applause). Although the oldest Faculty he would say that they had not yet reached the age of senility, and as a sign of strength he might say that most of their Professors had received the training in the McGill School. (Loud applause).

Mr. Fleet gave a song in an admirable manner.

Hon Justice JOHNSON, then proposed the toast of " Canada " as follows :—

Mr. President and gentlemen of the Graduates Society of McGill,—I beg leave to propose the toast of " Canada," (Cheers). You have heard to-night a great deal about your University, perhaps not too much, but you still have a little time to think of your country. The ringing cheer that greets the word shows me it goes straight to your hearts, as it ought to do. I shall make no apologetic preface. If I am not fit to speak somehow to such a toast, I ought to be ashamed of myself, for I am a Canadian to my heart's core. The degree of fitness is another matter. As to that I shall make no apologies either. If I fail to say what I wish, it is not for want of will to thank the Almighty for all His mercies to myself and to this my country, in which I have lived so long, nor yet for want of desire to say what I feel. As to all this, however, my only words shall be that it is my pride to be here; my regret that I should be no worthier. None of course can feel more pride in Canada than Canadians themselves; and, among Canadians, allow me to contend that none have so much right to be proud of the name as those who, not by accident or the act of others, but by their own selection, have made this their home. In a new and rapidly advancing country like ours, the population must naturally and of course consist not only of the natives of the soil, but also of the natives of other parts of the Empire, to say nothing of the rest of the world; so we may all call ourselves Canadians either voluntary or indigenous. My children have the comparative disadvantage of belonging only to the latter class. I, myself, feel the superiority of being a Canadian by my own choice. The Dominion of Canada is only one of the members—however important a one—of the vast Colonial Empire of England—an Empire presenting by its mere extent a spectacle never seen in the world before, and possessing probably a power quite immeasurable under conditions of cohesion and co-operation that are conceivable, and that have been indeed already conceived and expressed by some minds that have given the subject attention. It presents, also, certain features of anomaly, and, perhaps, of difficulty and danger, which may require all the sagacity and courage of the men of the present day to encounter and overcome. It presents the spectacle of a number of greater or lesser, but for the most part of self-governing communities, each asserting and practising sovereign rights, not only in its own territory, but as regards each other and as regards the parent state itself; for the power of taxing is of course a sovereign power in the sense I am speaking of, and it is exercised, not only against strangers, but against the other children of the same family and also against the head of the family itself. But it is a power, nevertheless, that appears to be necessary, not only because we must pay the expenses of self-government, but because God and nature have laid upon us the inevitable obligation of making a country for ourselves; and unless we are recreant and supine, instead of patient and brave, we will at last, and by Heaven's blessing, achieve the task. To make a decent start in life, and to create a home, is the natural, the reasonable and the honourable aim of most young men. The duty may be as great with a nation as with an individual; the difficulties may be greater, or at least on a larger scale; but one thing certain in both cases is, that life is made up of what are called difficulties, and character consists in overcoming them with dignity. A voice I shall never hear on earth again once said to me, when I was very young, "Any fool can swim with the current; but it takes a man indeed to swim against it," words which I have never forgotten, and which you may perhaps now take to heart better than I have done. Difficulties indeed! What are our difficulties compared with those of the glorious races in our motherland, in rearing for themselves the political liberties which, through the blood and the tears, and the unflinching courage, and the ardent prayers, and the willing deaths of our fathers, at last took shape in the fabric of the British constitution! That constitution may be said in a general way to be ours, though it is not quite so certain that with the form we also have the substance and reality of it. We may have one as good, and better too perhaps with reference to our different condition. All that I will not stop to debate now; but the English constitution as known to history we have not, any more than we have the English civilization of the present day; for the modern outcome of the mediæval, the feudal, the ecclesiastical, the commercial and the military spirit which make up to-day the constitution and the civilization of England, is a very complex thing indeed, and a very different one from the broad and simple democracy of Canada. I do not, as I said before, venture to stop a moment to discuss which is the better for us—we have no choice; but I only note the difference, and wish to avoid the mistake of confusing in all respects two things that are different in many, different in the stuff they are made of, different because in England there is a distinct and well marked line between classes and ranks, the result of feudal and other causes, while here, for better or for worse, we are all of one class, all of the people. Whether a constitution of historical growth and adaptation in an old country can be successfully transplanted by statute into a new country under very different conditions, is one of the problems of the future. It reminds me sometimes of the plum-puddings of my youth, in the great Northwest, in the days of its complete isolation from the rest of the world. Once a year, at least, in those days, every one must needs have his plum-pudding; but some of the good things puddings are usually made of were sometimes not to be had, but it was plum-pudding all the same; it was our plum-pudding; it was the best that was to be had; it was all we could get, and we made the best of it, and very jolly we were, and probably slept all the better for not loading our stomachs with all the precious stuff, which in strictness, I believe, usually enters into the constitution of historical plum-pudding. So let us make the best, say I, of our political constitution here; if it must not be called the English constitution, let us call it something that is, perhaps, better for us; let us call it by its right name, a Canadian constitution; and let us do our best to be happy under it! Yes, we are Canadians, and we are sometimes called, and with an ill concealed sneer, something more dreadful still—we have been called "Colonists," and not merely to express the fact—for that is undeniable—but to impute inferiority. It would be mere affectation to deny that we have often—not very often I hope, still too often—been spoken of disparagingly by even public writers for the English press—I don't say of eminence, but prominence is probably the better word—that sort of prominence that never allows modesty to stand in its way, the self-seekers, the smart writers of editorials for sale on the streets, the pushing nobodies with which populous cities, of course, abound. I suppose you have never been very sensitive about that sort of thing, and, on my part, I am convinced that it is neither common nor genuine; it is swagger, pure, simple and snobbish, swagger of the same kind that used to make silly people say, and probably believe, some half a century ago, that one Englishman was worth three Frenchmen. Of course, to reason with such people would be absurd, and they themselves, I am sure, would be puzzled if you asked them to mention the precise sort of inferiority they mean. Superiority both in kind and in degree there, of course, is; inferiority, undeniable and beyond all comparison, in respect, for instance, of national power, commercial wealth and, above all, in learning and culture. But England's history is ours as well as her's, and so are the riches of her example and the pride of her achievements. And when we come to inferiority of another kind—the inferiority clearly implied in these occasional and foolish insults—it is, as a little examination will show, as entirely unfounded and completely contrary to actual and historical truth, as the imputation itself is opposed to the taste and manners for which we naturally turn to imperial example. It is no pleasure to look back at the instances of conflict between Great Britain and her colonies; they are assuredly no matter of exultation on either side, but, if the truth must be told, it is plain matter of fact, nevertheless, that if you take the history of the last century or a little more—for before that the colonies were almost nothing, if you take say from the time of Bunker's Hill down to Majuba, England has never been beaten at all, as far as I remember, except by her colonists! Come down to more peaceful struggles! the cricket field and the water, who has ever beaten England at the bat, or with the oar, unless it be her own colonists? So that, after all, perhaps, if we had no better taste than some of them on the other side of the water, instead of being snubbed, we might be tempted to boast with the famed Kentuckian: "My father can lick 'most any man, and I can lick my father!" To speak seriously,

we must not allow such things to irritate even the youngest of us. Englishmen are not all snobs, and England has not been an unkind or an ungenerous parent to us. She has made mistakes, and will make more; but as a rule, when her children take ship and go beyond the sea to make "Greater Britains," she watches them—she does not let anybody bully them, and she helps them all she can consistently with the overwhelming cares of her immense family at home, crowded nowadays into a dear old house, which, I fear, is found very small to hold so many. Then, on the other hand, if we claim a share in her name and fame, we also remember the legal maxim : "*Nemo potest exuere patriam.*" We can't help being Englishmen if we would, and we wouldn't if we could. Englishmen in the true and honorable sense—Englishmen by right of inheritance of her liberties and by the spirit to preserve them, and if, as an old motto once familiar in many a Canadian household used to say, we have only changed skies and not hearts in coming over the sea. Do we not feel her sorrows and her trials, as well as share her history and her glory? Of course we do; and speaking tenderly and with submission on such a subject, I believe that at this hour that not in old England alone, but in many homes of her children here, reverting to the glorious past, and looking at what she was and what she is now, there are those who athwart the gloom of atheism, of dynamite, the decline of parliament and of commercial morality, or even in childish and boastful military displays, feel neither enthusiasm nor even comfort in looking for the quiet, firm and reassuring figure of Britannia of old. A feeling of this sort will creep over one occasionally nowadays, and it found expression, I remember, not very long ago in some lines written on the death of poor old Carlyle :

"He liv'd through England's triumphs; but he heard
With dying ears the shudder of decline."

Let us not despond, however ; let us pray God that England may be England still, and better and stronger than ever. Let us, us in Canada and as Canadians especially, never say die, but as heirs of England's liberty and greatness go forward on the mission Heaven has set before us ! Our way has not, like hers, to be cut with the sword ; our rights need not be won by force in the field, nor cemented by death on the block. We have no need to grope in darkness, and without the light of science, in political, moral or material progress. What our fathers lived and died for we have got, and we have got what they never had, and, alas! have not now. We have got bright skies and fruitful and boundless fields, and you might take all the land in the dear old country and dump it down in one place in the Northwest without its ever being felt except as a very small and, I fear, a comparatively damp and useless spot in the midst of the waste of wealth of the surrounding prairies. Gentlemen, I have been too long; but you know I am taking my holiday, and when an old horse gets out of the shafts and on to the grass he is very likely to kick up his heels, even at the risk of being taken for an old donkey. Let me give you ' Canada,' God bless her! Do your duty to her! Let my final words be to exhort you with high aim, and stout hearts to do your duty to your country. My course is nearly run; yours is all before you. Run it joyfully, for the voice of a nation is calling to you to be great, and the laws of God are inviting you to be happy. Canada—God bless her!

Mr. GEOFFRION responded in French. If a Canadian from choice has such affection for our country, what should one feel who was born on the shores of the St. Lawrence? If Canada be not yet one of the greatest countries of the world, the day will soon come when it will be such. And speaking among the graduates of this University, I feel there are the elements that will make us a great country. The motto of this University, "*Grandescunt aucta labore*," applies equally to Canada. Our country will grow. The various races that compose our people are a source of its strength. I recognize with pleasure that at a meeting composed entirely of English Canadians on Saturday night, Prof. Robidoux, a French gentleman, was unanimously elected President of this society. (Great cheers.) And thus we are all Canadians. Our predecessors have broken the soil, it is our part to work it. We have a lever put in our hands, our graduates are the force that must wield the lever. If our strength is exerted in a good way it will lead to progress, wealth and greatness. The progress must be directed by the universities. In Russia even the nihilists are moved from the universities. But in our country where freedom reigns, the universities must still govern, but never will in the direction of nihilism or communism. In industrial matters we are sometimes told that protection may even stimulate production, but if intellectual produce, there can never be over-production never a lack of consumers. I have

spoken chiefly of McGill, but I have a word to say about the supposed effort to draw off our alliance. Gentlemen, the thing is impossible. We are graduates of McGill. McGill is the first university. But McGill is not afraid of competition. We used to have a war of races, now we want competion, or as Americans would say, a race of races. We Latins want to show that though we are outstripped in wealth we claim not to be inferior in the intellectual realm. And McGill has recognized this in conferring the degree of Doctor of Laws on Mr. Frechette, our French-Canadian poet. (Cheers.)

Mr. Geoffrion closed by a few words in English and resumed his seat amid applause.

Mr. ROSWELL FISHER also replied to the toast of Canada, and thought himself a worthy Canadian as far as his aspirations for Canada were concerned. Their's was a big country though not widely known beyond its borders; though a big country, it had yet to become a great country; individual and national character was wanted. He urged them to make their country a greater Britain and to be themselves greater Britions [applause].

Rev. Dr. STEVENSON, in proposing the health of the Press, said he would not venture upon what Carlyle had called "Satan's Invisible World Displayed," [laughter], but would say that the Press was at least prolific in news and in the creation of new atitudes of language; where fact ended, imagination began, and news, whether true or not, was always more or less striking. [Applause]. Seriously, the Press was a great power in the diffusion of knowledge, which was the safeguard of liberty. The reverend gentleman resumed his seat amidst great cheering, and was followed by

Mr. FAUCHETTE, replying in French to the toast of ' The Press,' said it was the third time he had had the misfortune, if he might call it so, to speak after the able speakers who had proposed this toast. The most interesting speeches are the shortest. He then referred to the press as the great civilising agent of this century, and considered its greatest function was to spread the light of science and save from the rocks that wrecks the mariners on the coast.

Dr. KELLY having proposed " Absent Friends," and " The Ladies " having been duly honored, the company dispersed after singing " Auld Lang Syne," all pronouncing the dinner a most marked success.